Spencer

Love,

Mark & Lana
Russell

BABAR'S
BUSY YEAR

BABAR'S
BUSY YEAR

Laurent de Brunhoff

Harry N. Abrams, Inc., Publishers

Babar, Celeste, and their daughter Isabelle go for a walk through the forest.

"Look!" cries Isabelle. "The leaves have turned red and yellow. And they are starting to fall."

"Yes," says Babar. "Autumn is here."

The air is cool and tingly now.

The older children play soccer, but Isabelle loves hopscotch. She is so absorbed in her game, she does not notice the little squirrel gathering acorns nearby.

For a special treat, the children visit a pumpkin patch. Isabelle finds the biggest pumpkin of all. Arthur will have to carry it home for her.

Pom picks a whole basket of apples.
Flora gathers corn.

Alexander carves a pumpkin.
What a spooky face!

Winter has come to Celesteville.

"Come play with us!" the children shout to Cornelius.

"No," he tells them. "It is too cold for me."

Cornelius prefers to read by the fire.
The Old Lady keeps him company.

Babar's family goes to the mountains
for the holidays. They enjoy skiing and sledding.
Look at all that snow! Winter seems like it
will last forever.

But before you know it, spring is here. The cherry trees burst into bloom.

Celesteville is full of beautiful flowers.
Arthur picks some daffodils.

Zephir arranges some tulips.

Isabelle finds a nest
of baby birds.

Babar loves to work in the garden. Flora and Pom help their father plant flowers.

"Look, Mama! It is starting to rain," says Isabelle.

Celeste laughs. "Now we will not need the hose and watering can!"

The days turn sunny and warm. Summer has come to Celesteville. The children like to have picnics by the lake.

After lunch they play.
Isabelle finds a grasshopper.

Flora tries to catch
a butterfly.

"It is so hot," Pom says. "We
should go swimming!"

That is just what everyone does.
"Watch out below!" cries Alexander
as he jumps into the water.

Soon the family must go home.
"I wish summer would last forever," says Arthur.

"Not me!" Isabelle tells him.

"I want fall to come again, so I can go to school.
I cannot wait!"

Designed by Vivian Cheng
Production Manager: Jonathan Lopes

Library of Congress Cataloging-in-Publication Data:

Brunhoff, Laurent de, 1925–
Babar's busy year / Laurent de Brunhoff.
p. cm.
Summary: The changing seasons bring new
delights to Babar and his friends in Celesteville.
ISBN 0-8109-5864-3
[1. Seasons—Fiction. 2. Elephants—Fiction.] I. Title.

PZ7.B82843Babk 2005
[E]—dc22
2004012652

Printed and bound in China
10 9 8 7 6 5 4 3 2 1

Harry N. Abrams, Inc.
100 Fifth Avenue
New York, NY 10011
www.abramsbooks.com

Abrams is a subsidiary of LA MARTINIÈRE
GROUPE